DATE DUE		
NOV 1 9 2011			
MAY 1 3 2013			

First Time

Going to a Restaurant

Melinda Radabaugh

Heinemann Library
Chicago, Illinois

Customer Service 888-454-2279
Visit our website at www.heinemannlibrary.com

Designed by Sue Emerson, Heinemann Library
Printed and bound in the United States by Lake Book Manufacturing, Inc.

07 06 05 04 03
10 9 8 7 6 5 4 3 2 1

Library of Congress Cataloging-in-Publication Data
Radabaugh, Melinda Beth.
  Going to a restaurant / Melinda Beth Radabaugh.
      v. cm. — (First time)
Includes index.
Contents: What is a restaurant? — What kinds of restaurants are there?— Where will you go? — Who works in a restaurant? — What is on the table? — What do you do in a restaurant? — How do you get your food? — Who cooks the food? — What happens after your meal?
  ISBN 1-4034-0226-4 (HC), 1-4034-0465-8 (Pbk.)
  1. Restaurants—Juvenile literature. [1. Restaurants.] I. Title. II. Series.
  TX945 .R27 2002
  647.95--dc21

                                        2002001158

Acknowledgments
The author and publishers are grateful to the following for permission to reproduce copyright material:
pp. 4, 5, 8, 9, 10R, 12, 13, 14, 15, 16, 17, 20, 21 Robert Lifson/Heinemann Library; p. 6 Kevin Fleming/Corbis; p. 7T David Tumley/Corbis; p. 7B AJA Productions/ImageBank/Getty Images; p. 10L Leslie O'Shaughnessy/Visuals Unlimited; p. 11L Amor Montes De Oca; p. 11R Herve Donnezan/Photo Researchers; p. 18 Owen Franken/Corbis; p. 19L Eric Futran/FoodPix; p. 19R Guido Cozzi/Bruce Coleman; p. 22 (row 1, L–R) Erwin C. "Bud" Nielsen/Visuals Unlimited, Heinemann Library; p. 22 (row 2, L–R) PhotoDisc, John A. Rizzo/PhotoDisc; p. 22 (row 3, L–R) Robert Lifson/Heinemann Library, RDF/Visuals Unlimited; p. 23 (row 1, L–R) Robert Lifson/Heinemann Library, Erwin C. "Bud" Nielsen/Visuals Unlimited, Robert Lifson/Heinemann Library, Owen Franken/Corbis; p. 23 (row 2, L–R) Herve Donnezan/Photo Researchers, Leslie O'Shaughnessy/Visuals Unlimited, Robert Lifson/Heinemann Library, Robert Lifson/Heinemann Library; p. 23 (row 3, L–R) Eric Futran/FoodPix, Robert Lifson/Heinemann Library, Guido Cozzi/Bruce Coleman, Heinemann Library; p. 23 (row 4) Robert Lifson/Heinemann Library; p. 24 (top, L–R) Erwin C. "Bud" Nielsen/Visuals Unlimited, Heinemann Library; p. 24B John A. Rizzo/PhotoDisc; back cover (L–R) Herve Donnezan/Photo Researchers, Erwin C. "Bud" Nielsen/Visuals Unlimited

Cover photograph by Robert Lifson/Heinemann Library
Photo Research by Amor Montes de Oca

Special thanks to our advisory panel for their help in the preparation of this book:

Eileen Day, Preschool Teacher
Chicago, IL

Ellen Dolmetsch,
Library Media Specialist
Wilmington, DE

Kathleen Gilbert,
Second Grade Teacher
Round Rock, TX

Sandra Gilbert,
Library Media Specialist
Houston, TX

Angela Leeper,
Educational Consultant
North Carolina Department
of Public Instruction
Raleigh, NC

Pam McDonald,
Reading Support Specialist
Winter Springs, FL

Melinda Murphy,
Library Media Specialist
Houston, TX

Special thanks to the Lee family and the Hong Kong Café, Amy Ng, and the Chan family for their assistance with the photographs in this book.

Some words are shown in bold, **like this.**
You can find them in the picture glossary on page 23.

Contents

What Is a Restaurant?

A restaurant is a place to eat.

You can choose the food you will eat.

Someone brings the food to you.

You pay for your **meal**.

What Kinds of Restaurants Are There?

Some restaurants have foods you eat at home.

Some have foods that may be different.

At some restaurants, people dress up.

At others, people wear everyday clothes.

Where Are Restaurants?

Some restaurants are near your house.

You can walk there.

Other restaurants may be far away.

You go there in a car.

Who Works in a Restaurant?

A **host** shows you where to sit.

A **bus person** pours water.

A **server** takes your **order**.

A **chef** makes the food.

What Is on the Table?

There is a **tablecloth** on the table.

There are **napkins** and glasses, too.

There are forks and knives.

This table has spoons and **chopsticks,** too.

What Do You Do in a Restaurant?

First, you read the **menu**.

It shows the foods you may eat there.

Next, the **server** takes your **order**.

Then, you wait for your food.

How Do You Get Your Food?

The **server** writes down your **order**.

The server gives the order to the kitchen.

Soon your food is ready!

The server brings it on a **tray**.

Who Cooks the Food?

A **chef** cooks the food.

Chefs cook on a big **stove**.

Chef's helpers cut vegetables.

A pastry chef makes desserts.

What Happens After Your Meal?

You might eat **dessert**.

Then, a **bus person** takes away your plates.

You put money on the table
for the **server.**

You pay for your **meal** and
go home.

Quiz

What can you find on a **menu?**

Look for the answers on page 24.

Picture Glossary

bus person
pages 10, 20

dessert
pages 19, 20

napkin
page 12

stove
page 18

chef
pages 11, 18

host
page 10

order
pages 11, 15, 16

tablecloth
page 12

chef's helpers
page 19

meal
pages 5, 21

pastry chef
page 19

tray
page 17

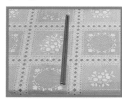

chopsticks
page 13

menu
page 14, 22

server
pages 11, 15, 16, 17, 21

Note to Parents and Teachers

Reading for information is an important part of a child's literacy development. Learning begins with a question about something. Help children think of themselves as investigators and researchers by encouraging their questions about the world around them. Each chapter in this book begins with a question. Read the question together. Look at the pictures. Talk about what you think the answer might be. Then read the text to find out if your predictions were correct. Think of other questions you could ask about the topic, and discuss where you might find the answers. Assist children in using the picture glossary and the index to practice new vocabulary and research skills.

Index

Answers to quiz on page 22

dessert

salad

pizza